William Henry Holmes, George Amos Dorsey

Observations on a Collection of Papuan Crania

Vol. 21

William Henry Holmes, George Amos Dorsey

Observations on a Collection of Papuan Crania
Vol. 21

ISBN/EAN: 9783337336073

Printed in Europe, USA, Canada, Australia, Japan

Cover: Foto ©Andreas Hilbeck / pixelio.de

More available books at **www.hansebooks.com**

PUBLICATIONS

OF THE

FIELD COLUMBIAN MUSEUM.

ANTHROPOLOGICAL SERIES

VOLUME II.

CHICAGO, U. S. A.
1897·1903*

*For date of issue of each paper see Table of Contents.

TABLE OF CONTENTS.

Field Columbian Museum

Publication 21.

Anthropological Series. Vol. II, No. 1.

OBSERVATIONS ON A COLLECTION OF PAPUAN CRANIA

BY

George A. Dorsey,

Assistant Curator, Department of Anthropology.

WITH NOTES ON

PRESERVATION AND DECORATIVE FEATURES

BY

William H. Holmes,

Curator, Department of Anthropology.

Chicago, U. S. A

August, 1897.

OBSERVATIONS

ON A

COLLECTION OF PAPUAN CRANIA.

By George A. Dorsey.

WITH NOTES ON

PRESERVATION and DECORATIVE FEATURES.

By William H. Holmes.

CONTENTS.

ILLUSTRATIONS.

OBSERVATIONS ON A COLLECTION OF PAPUAN CRANIA, BY GEORGE A. DORSEY.

INTRODUCTION.

While considerable numbers of crania from New Guinea have been described, and while the type of the Papuan is fairly well determined, it has seemed that the collection which furnishes the basis of this essay combines a sufficient number of characters to make its description of interest and importance. In the first place the skulls come from a single locality, having been received from a native chief who used them for the adornment of his house and prized them, it is said, as trophies of war. In the second place each skull has been decorated in the frontal region by designs in incised lines, and the jaws are bound to the skull by bandages which pass through the nares around the symphysis, and around the zygoma through a hole in the ramus just beneath the sigmoid notch.

No attempt has been made to compare the results obtained in the present examination with those of previous investigators. This is to be regretted, but the available literature on the subject is not sufficient to make the undertaking at all satisfactory.* This being the case only the facts which have been obtained by observation have been recorded. In the first part there is a somewhat detailed description of each skull, the collection being divided according to sex, then follows a summary in which the two sexes are contrasted and averages for the entire series given, together with a table of measurements and plates. There is finally, in the second part, a description of the frontal carvings and the bandages by Prof. W. H. Holmes, to whom I am much indebted for consenting to undertake this work, and to whom I herewith offer my sincerest thanks.

As may be seen, the collection comprises sixteen skulls, distributed as follows: males, eight; females, seven; child, one. Apart from the child's skull there is very little discrepancy in the age of the

*This does not mean, however, that I have made no use of the standard works on anthropology, and I wish to take this opportunity to express my sense of obligation to that most valuable monograph on skulls, " The Report on Human Crania," by Sir William Turner, in the Xth volume of the Challenger Report.

crania. The average may be put at about thirty-five to forty years,
but one skull having the basilar synchondrosis open, and none of
them showing any signs of considerable age.

In regard to the measurements taken, only those have been
adopted which are in general use by craniologists. Concerning the
methods employed but few words are necessary. The cranial capacity is taken with No. 8 shot, after the directions of Broca, as
described in detail by Topinard in his "Elements d'Anthropologie."
It should be borne in mind, however, that, as E. Schmidt has pointed
out, although the method of Broca, when conscientiously conducted,
reduces the "personal" element to a minimum, its results are in
excess of the true capacity ; and Schmidt has tabulated the percent-
age of error, so that it is possible by making the proper deduction to
arrive at a correct result. As the majority of observers, however,
have given their results as originally found by Broca's method, I have
allowed my results to stand without alteration.

The weight is recorded in ounces, and is merely given to show
sexual and individual variation. The maximum length is taken from
the glabella. For the facial diameters I have not followed the most
common usage, but in both cases have started from nasion. This,
of course, does not give the true diameter of the length of the
face; but it does limit the factor of possible error on the part
of the observer. The dental index is after the formula of Professor Flower. Other references to methods and measurements will
be found in the text, especially in the general summary. While the
fact that the lower jaw is held in place by bandages is of great interest to the ethnologist, it prevents in most cases any careful study of
the condition of the hard palate, or of the variations in the size or
cusps of the teeth. For this reason no attempt has been made to
measure the hard palate, or to pursue any definite detailed series of
observations of the lower jaw. It may also be noted here that in
almost every case the interior nares have been destroyed by the bandages; this destruction generally included the lachrymals and the
greater portion of the ethmoid bone, so that here also we are deprived
of studying the individual variations in the lachrymal, one of the most
interesting, although the smallest, bone in the face.

I.

CRANIOLOGICAL OBSERVATIONS.

A. MALE CRANIA.

NO. 40,617.—Skull of adult male, large, massive and heavy. Cranial capacity, 1,515 cc. The upper incisors and right third molar and lower right second premolar have been lost; their alveoli are still open. All the other teeth are present, in sound, healthy condition, but somewhat worn. (No. 2 of Broca's scale.)

NORMA FRONTALIS.—(See Pl. I, Fig. 1.) Frontal region moderately well developed; not prominent; minimum frontal width, 103 mm. The glabella is entirely obscured by the highly projecting broad superciliary ridges. The orbits are quadrilateral in outline, with a decided downward inclination to their axes. The inferior and outer orbital margins are not sharp or even well-defined, but rounded so that it is difficult to locate with absolute exactness the external inferior angle of the orbit, or even of the neighboring margins. The nasal bones are long and well fashioned. There is a slight concavity from nasion to the level of the vascular foramen, where the nasals become slightly convex. The bridge is only moderately well marked. The nasal opening is almost sloping, at any rate it is rather more than rounded; spine very insignificant. The canine fossæ are much fuller than is usual in this series. The malar tuberosities are not prominent, nor are the zygomatic arches outstanding. Alveolar arch long and full.

NORMA VERTICALIS.—(See Pl. I, Fig. 2.) The skull is extremely long and narrow, measuring 191 x 131 mm., with a cephalic index of 68. The parietal eminences are fairly prominent and outstanding. The temporal fossæ are exceptionally broad and deep, and the inferior temporal line approaches within 40 mm. of the sagittal suture, and follows the course of the lambdoidal for nearly half its length.

NORMA POSTERIOR.—(See Pl. II, Fig. 1.) The pentagon is well marked; the angle at the vertex is sharp and distinct, the base is horizontal, with nearly straight sides; the asterionic diameter is 100 mm., being exceeded by the maximum breadth diameter by 31 mm.

9

On each parietal bone, beginning about half way down the sagittal suture, begins a broad groove which extends downwards and ends in the lambdoidal suture just below lambda. Seen in profile the two grooves are very plain, with the sagittal suture at a median elevation between them.

NORMA LATERALIS.—(See Pl. II, Fig. 2.) The curve of the vault of the cranium may be divided into five regions: from ophryon to metopion, from metopion to obelion with a very slight depression just posterior to bregma, from obelion to lambda, from lambda to inion, and from inion to opisthion. The frontal development is fairly good; the vertex is somewhat horizontal; there is a sharp break in the curve at obelion and the occipital point is half way between lambda and inion. There is a large amount of alveolar prognathism, the teeth also have a strong forward projection. The malar bone is excluded from the spheno-maxillary fissure by the articulation of the sphenoid with the inferior maxillary bone. The temporal border of the malar bone is prominently marked.

NORMA BASALIS.— (See Pl. III, Fig. 1.) The foramen magnum is long and narrow, measures 36 x 25 mm.; its plane is directed backwards. The condyles are far forward, slightly oblique, and encroach somewhat on the anterior border of the foramen magnum. The basilar process is long and narrow, with deep, well-defined pharingeal and navicular fossæ. The right foramen spinosum has its posterior border open into the spheno-petrossal fissure, while the foramen ovale is a mere slit-like opening. The posterior condylar foramina are absent. There are two right and one left mastoid foramina. Palate is long and narrow, U-shaped, and is 18 mm. deep in parts; there is a gradual slope to the incisor alveoli. The roof of the palate is rough and thrown into irregular folds. The postglenoid processes are heavily developed. •

SUTURES.—The coronal is exceedingly simple, the lambdoidal is slightly complex, and the sagittal is very deeply but coarsely serrated. The coronal suture in places has begun to synostose. There is an epipteric bone at right pterion, and it is difficult to determine if it corresponds to the upper angle of the alisphenoid or is an extra bone; it cannot belong to the temporal or parietal. On the left side the temporal is 10 mm. from the frontal bone. The malo-maxillary suture is synostosed and almost obliterated.

PROCESSES.—The mastoids are short, thick and massive. Styloid processes small. The sphenoidal spines are long and unusually thick. The external pterygoid plates are both broken; the internal

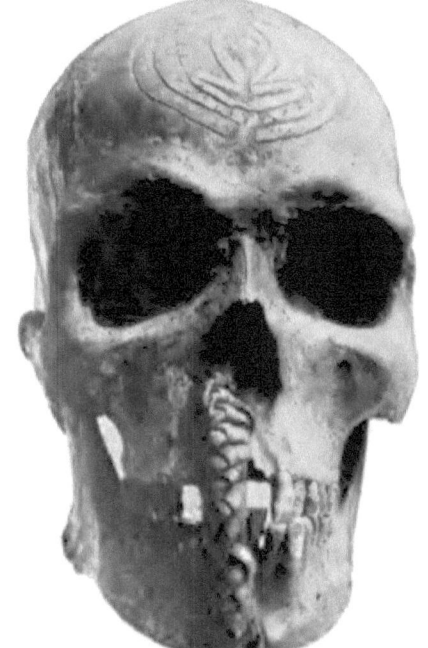

FIG. 1.

FIG. 2.
PL. I. TWO VIEWS OF MALE SKULL, NO. 40,617.

plates are narrow with long hamular processes.   External angular process of frontal, broad and long.

MUSCULAR IMPRESSIONS.— Prominently indicated.   The long temporal line has already been noted; on its frontal aspect is a well-developed crest.   The external occipital crest is not individualized, but is included in the *torus occipitalis transversus* which extends from asterion to asterion, and is 22 mm. wide and 8 mm. high through the region of inion.

LOWER JAW.— Massive and strongly fashioned.   Through the region of the internal oblique line the body measures 18 mm. in thickness.   The attachment ridges of the masseter and external pterygoid muscles are heavy and rough.   The ascending ramus is 34 mm. in breadth and the condyloid height is 70 mm.   The coronoid process is broad, but not sharp, and curves backwards.   The mental protuberance and tubercles are not prominent.   Height of symphysis, 33 mm.; mandibular angle, 110°.

NO. 40,619.—Skull of an adult male, heavy and compact, but small.   The lachrymals and interior nares are destroyed.   Cranial capacity, 1,285 cc.   The following teeth are *in situ:* upper left first and second molars, and right canine and first premolar; lower left second molar and right lateral incisor and second and third molars.   These teeth are perfectly sound and not worn.   The alveoli of the other teeth are in sound condition, except those of the right first and second molars.   A large amount of absorption has taken place in this region and simply the dwarfed crests of the alveoli remain, while the maxillary sinus has been opened in three different places.   A large amount of absorption has also gone on in the labial margin of the alveoli of both right and left lower first molars.

NORMA FRONTALIS.— Forehead retreating and extremely narrow; minimum frontal width, 87 mm.   Glabella prominent, with supraorbital ridges.   Orbits squarish, with decidedly oblique axes.   Nasals long and slender with slight convexity from above downwards, and rather sharply arched.   Nasal openings rounded, with single and very diminutive anterior spine and well-developed incisor crest.   The incisor fossæ are slightly sunken; malar tuberosities prominent; zygomatic arches appressed.   Entire face appears long and narrow.

NORMA VERTICALIS.— Ovoid; frontal development slight, with no indication of frontal eminences; parietal eminences fairly well developed, but asymmetrical in position, that of the right side being situated about 15 mm. forward of the left.   The skull is pronouncedly phænozygous, the fronto-zygomatic index being 75.

NORMA POSTERIOR.—Well marked pentagonal form, broad through the parietal tubera, sides longer than the base, with well marked vertical angle. There is only a difference of 19 mm. between the asterionic diameter and the maximum cranial diameter.

NORMA LATERALIS.—The curve is gradual from ophryon to within about 25 mm. of obelion; the curve is more rapid then till just below lambda, which is the most posterior point of the skull; the portion from inion to opisthion is almost horizontal. Deep depression at nasion with a considerable amount of alveolar as well as facial prognathism. The temporal fossa is broad and long, the superior line extending within 45 mm. of the sagittal suture just behind bregma, within 50 mm. of lambda, and within 45 mm. of inion. The direction of the left temporo-parietal suture is almost straight, except for a slight curve just above its junction with the supra-mastoid crest, the right suture is even more nearly a straight line. Left pterion is formed by a frontal process of the temporal bone, which joins the frontal to an extent of 7 mm. Right pterion approaches a K.

NORMA INFERIOR.—Foramen magnum almost circular, measures 36 x 33 mm. The condyles are placed far forward and almost meet in the median line. The plane of the foramen magnum is directed considerably forward, so much so that the occipital angle of Broca is 22° The basilar process is narrow and measures 21 mm. in length; the pharingeal tubercle is well marked, with deep navicular fossa. On the left side the foramen ovale is almost circular in outline, and the foramen spinosum is situated almost at the tip of the spinous process, which on this side projects backward beyond the glasserian fissure. The more normal condition prevails on the right side; but the external pterygoid plate is connected with the spinous process by a bony spiculum which passes over the foramen ovale and just to the inside of the foramen lacerum. The glenoid fossæ are not deep, but long and narrow from side to side. The palate has a decided U-shape, and is comparatively shallow.

SUTURES.—Coronal extremely simple; sagittal and lambdoidal rather complex. The coronal suture is synostosed and obliterated below stephanion; the sagittal is obliterated in its anterior two-fifths, and throughout its inner portion is firmly synostosed, the lambdoidal is partially synostosed. The upper half of the nasal suture is ankylosed.

PROCESSES.—Mastoids of medium size, small internal pterygoids, but external pterygoids broad, with deep pterygoid fossæ. The external angular process of the frontal bone is unusually long but not so massive as in some other skulls of this collection.

FIG. 1.

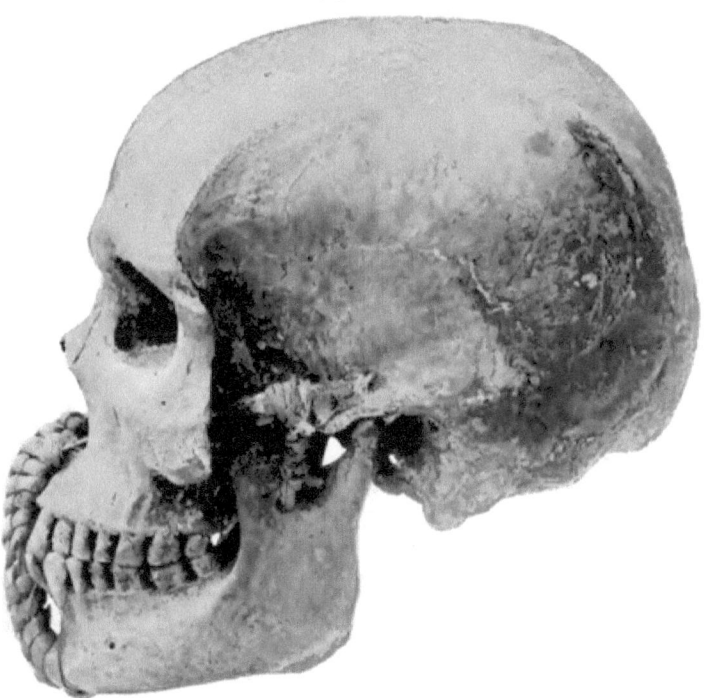

FIG. 2.
PL. II. TWO VIEWS OF MALE SKULL. NO. 4,617.

Muscular Impressions.—The temporal line is well marked throughout its course, but is not especially rough.   The external occipital protuberance broadens out in a heavy transverse mass, forming a well-defined torus occipitalis transversus.

Mandible.—Of rather delicate and feeble dimensions.   The condyles are long and narrow and taper to a sharp point on their inner termination.   The sigmoid notch is shallow with short thin coronoid processes.   The ramus is narrow and 62 mm. in height; the muscular insertions for both masseter and pterygoid are very pronounced. The body is thin and shallow except for the internal oblique line. The mental protuberance is not prominent, with mental tubercles in a corresponding degree of development.   Mandibular angle 115°, height of symphysis 30 mm.

No. 40,614.—Skull of adult male.   The interior nares including lachrymals have been destroyed.   Cranial capacity, 1,415 cc.   Only the following teeth are *in situ:* the lower molars, the upper left first molar, and the right canine, first premolar and first molar.   These teeth are in perfect condition and show no trace of wear.   The alveoli of the other teeth are sound.   In addition to the foregoing remarks about the teeth it is to be specially noted, that between the lower premolar of the right side, a third premolar has made its appearance and is just on a level with the alveolus.   It can only be seen from its buccal side.

Norma Frontalis.—The forehead is fully developed, and the frontal eminences are more prominent than they generally are in the male series.   The glabella is full and round, with superciliary ridges less prominent.   The orbits are quadrilateral in form, with a decided downward inclination of the external part of the orbital arch.   The nasal bones are medium sized, asymmetrical, concave from above downward, and sharply arched.   Nasal openings rounded and spine weak.   The canine fossæ are deep and broad; tuberosity of the malars prominent with projecting zygomatic arches.

Norma Verticalis.—Slightly oval with pronounced parietal eminences, a squarish frontal termination and a highly projecting occiput. Bizygostephanic index 49.

Norma Posterior.—The pentagon is not as well marked as usual, for the base is broad and straight; the sides are almost equally straight, and the angle at the vertex is more open than usual.   The asterionic diameter is 116 mm. as compared with 133 mm. for the maximum breadth.

Norma Lateralis.—Well marked frontal curvature, with a decidedly prominent occipital tubercle.   At inion the curve changes rapidly in a forward direction, flattened somewhat over vertex. Zygomatic arches slender and delicate.   Pronounced alveolar prognathism.

NORMA INFERIOR.—Foramen-magnum elliptical, measures 34 x 28 mm.   The posterior borders of the condyles are much depressed—platybasic deformity.   On the right side the foramen spinosum opens into a backward slit-like prolongation of the foramen lacerum.   The apex of the left petrosal bone is defective and does not cover, except by a bony spiculum, any portion of the carotid canal.   The glenoid fossa is deep and slightly circular, and on the left side the condyle is almost at right angles to the glasserian fissure.   On both sides there is a well-defined postglenoid process.   The hard palate is hyperbolic in form, almost U-shaped, and is but 14 mm. in its deepest part, and slopes gradually to the incisor alveoli.

SUTURES.—The coronal is exceedingly simple, the sagittal is somewhat complex and the lambdoidal for the greater part is from 10 to 20 mm. in breadth and is extremely complicated throughout its length by wormian bones.   These begin at lambda as large simple bones, but toward asterion on both sides they become long and narrow, or replaced by numerous ossicles.   At left asterion there are two large and two small individual wormian bones.   Synostosis has begun in all the sutures in the region of pterion.

PROCESSES.—The mastoids are moderately sized.   The left is rather more rounded than the right, which is slightly compressed from side to side.   The digastric and occipital grooves are very shallow.   The external pterygoid plate is much below the average in size, while the internal plate is reduced to a mere crest-like spinous process.   The suture of the internal pterygoid is still open on its anterior and posterior aspects.

MUSCULAR IMPRESSIONS.— As a rule faint, inion is simply a roughened portion of the occipital protuberance.   The occipital lines are not ridges in any sense of the term, but rather swellings.   The temporal lines can be distinguished throughout their length but are not at all prominent.

MANDIBLE.—Small and weakly formed.   The condyles are short and broad to correspond to the form of the glenoid fossae.   There is a slight mental protuberance and but little trace of the tubercles. The sigmoid notch is broad and but slightly concave.   The coronoid process is almost pyramidal in shape owing to its thickness.   The mental foramina are immediately beneath the second premolars.

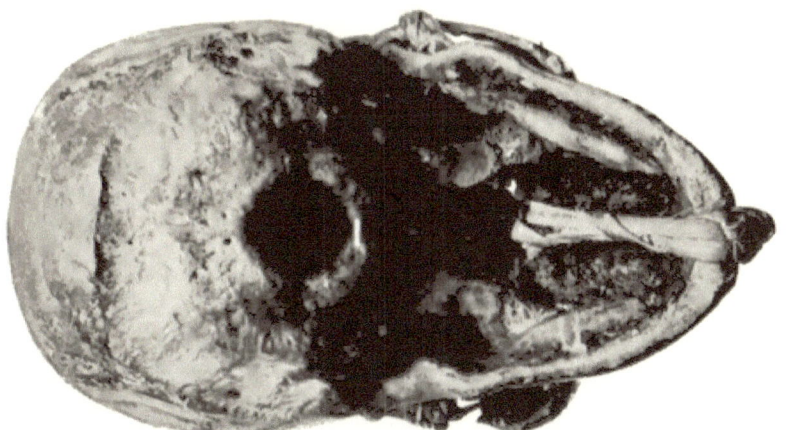

Fig. 1. (40,617.)

Fig. 2. (40,607.)

PL. III. VIEWS OF MALE AND FEMALE SKULLS, NOS. 40,617 AND 40,607.

Genio-glossal spine double; genio-hyoid crest very small. The stylo-hyoid ridge is heavily marked, especially that portion just under the first molars. Height of symphysis 31 mm.; mandibular angle 130°.

NO. 40,595.— Skull of an adult male.   Teeth all present in per-fect condition, with no sign of wear.   Cranial capacity, 1,390 cc.

Norma Frontalis.— (See Pl. IV, Fig. 1.)   Glabella and super-ciliary ridges prominent.   Orbits slightly rounded, with a very slight inclination of the axes.   Interorbital space medium.   There is pres-ent on both ridges the infra-orbital suture.   The nasal bones are small, well-shaped and form a projecting bridge; the nasal openings are fairly sloping with but little nasal spine.   The canine fossæ are deep, almost cavernous.   Malars and zygomatic arches projecting, but total face is long and narrow, especially in the region of the jaws.   .

Norma Verticalis.—The skull is long and narrow and of regular outline, owing to the slight development of both frontal and parietal eminences. Cephalic index, 65. Bizygostephanic index, 87.

Norma Posterior.— Pentagonal form with broad base and sides and rather angular at vertex.

Norma Lateralis.— (See Pl. IV, Fig. 2.)   Well-marked frontal development; the curve of the vertex is gradual to obelion, where it passes rapidly down to inion, there it becomes almost a straight line to opisthion.   The frontal external angular process is thick and heavy.   The glabella overhangs nasion to a considerable extent; alveolar prognathism marked.

Norma Inferior.—The foramen magnum is nearly circular, 31 x 28 mm., except on left side, where the posterior condyloid foramen is continuous with the foramen magnum.   On the right side the jugular process has grown over and covers the petro-occipital synchon-drosis.

Sutures.—The coronal and lambdoidal are very simple; the sagittal is slightly more complex.   There is a long, narrow wormian bone, 25 x 4 mm., at right pterion; also a small wormian bone just above right asterion.

There can still be made out a cleft, 11 mm. in length, starting just above left asterion and extending in the direction of inion; a somewhat similar cleft, but not so distinct, exists also on the right side.

Processes.—The mastoids are very rough and of large size, although not long.   The styloid processes are large and thick, and are protected by the vaginal sheath for a distance of about 15 mm.

MUSCULAR IMPRESSIONS.—Well marked throughout, especially in the occipital region where the curved lines and protuberances are extremely rough. The insertions for both the masseter and internal pterygoid muscles are strongly indicated.

MANDIBLE.—Strongly developed; height of symphysis, 31 mm.; mandibular angle, 120°. Very slight mental protuberances and no indication of mental tuberosities.

NO. 40,620.—Skull of an adult male of unusual size and weight. Cranial capacity, 1,560 cc. The lachrymals and interior nares are destroyed. The following teeth are *in situ:* upper canines and right premolars and left second premolar; lower second and third right molars and first and second left molars. These teeth are sound and very slightly worn. The upper third molars have never erupted. The alveoli of the other teeth are all sound, with but one exception. The exception is in the case of the lower right first molar and second premolar. There is a deep circular excavation here and the jaw has been fractured between these two teeth. The line of the fracture can still be plainly seen both on the labial and buccal side of the jaw, which has in its outer aspect a globular appearance.

NORMA FRONTALIS.—The face is broader and much fuller in the frontal region than usual. This is due both to the comparatively full development of the frontal tubera and to the absolute width of the frontal bone, the minimum diameter of which is 103 mm. The glabella is not prominent, yielding as a median depression between the sharp supraorbital crests. The orbits are long and narrow, with axes inclined to a considerable degree. The nasal bones are well formed, with prominent, acute bridge. The openings are round, with diminutive nasal spine. Canine fossæ somewhat depressed; long alveolar process, but not highly prognathic.

NORMA VERTICALIS.—While the length is about normal for these skulls, 187 mm., the maximum breadth is much above the average, being 140 mm. The parietal eminences are well indicated but not sharply rounded. The bizygostephanic index is 82—the highest of the series.

NORMA POSTERIOR.—The pentagonal form almost disappears in the very open angle of the vertex, the cranium being broader than it is high, and the maximum diameter exceeding that of the asterionic by only 34 mm.

NORMA LATERALIS.—The frontal development is very striking and ends anteriorly to bregma. From that point to half the distance of the sagittal suture the curve disappears entirely. The posterior two-

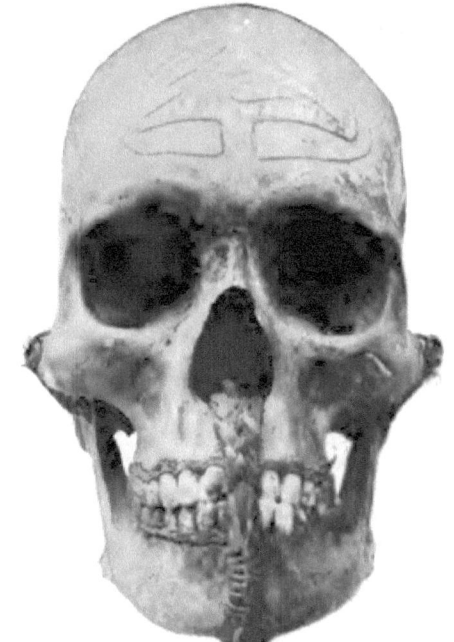

FIG. 1.

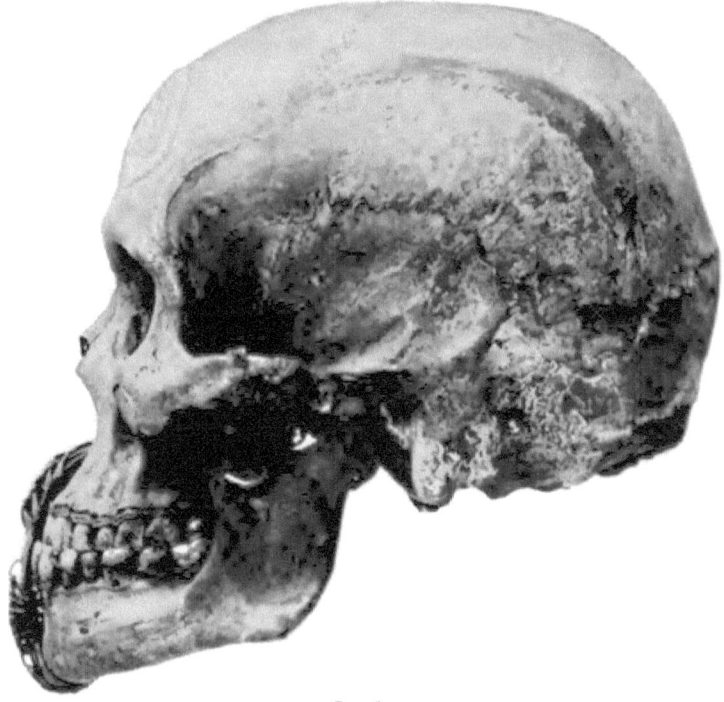

FIG. 2.
PL. IV. TWO VIEWS OF MALE SKULL, NO. 40,595.

thirds of the **sagittal curve is** rapidly downwards **to** near lambda, just above which **is a depression.** There is a **bulging** of the occipital squama between **lambda and inion; below inion** the curve is rapidly forward, forming an almost **horizontal plane.** The superior curved line projects about **5 mm.** in profile.

NORMA INFERIOR.—The foramen magnum is diamond shaped, with diameters of 34 **and 32** mm., **and looks** directly downward. The **right** jugular fossa **is** unusually large. The palate is **shallow and** U-shaped.

SUTURES.—The sutures are **all simple, especially the coronal;** this suture is almost obliterated below stephanion. **The sagittal and** lambdoidal **are** partially synostosed. There **is a** very large wormian bone in **both** left and right lambdoidal sutures near lambda, one at left **asterion and two at** right **asterion.** The spheno-parietal suture **on the left side is 17** mm. **in length; on the** right **side** it **is** 14 mm.

PROCESSES.—Mastoids small; **the external occipital** protuberance is **expanded laterally** into a torus **occipitalis transversus of the most** pronounced **type.**

MUSCULAR IMPRESSIONS.— Not heavy; as a **rule the surfaces** are smooth. There **is,** however, a very broad indented surface **for** the origin of the masseter.

MANDIBLE.— Of weak development **and of** large **dimensions to** correspond to the large inferior **expansion of** the face, **but the** body and ramus are small. The mental **protuberance and** tuberosities are **small.** Height of ramus 31 mm.

NO. 40,618.— Skull of adult male. Cranial **capacity,** 1,415 cc. The left incisors and canine teeth have been lost; their alveoli are in **perfect** condition. The third molars have never erupted either above or **below,** otherwise the teeth are perfectly sound and **show no trace** of wear. **Lachrymals and interior nares** destroyed.

NORMA FRONTALIS.— Long **narrow face with retreating** forehead and slight development **of** the frontal **eminences. Glabella** rounded with faint supraorbital ridges; **orbits squarish; narrow,** long nasal bones, with only slight convexity **but sharp** nasal bridge; spine small, incisor crest prominent and openings **of** anterior nares rounded There is present **on** both sides the infraorbital suture. Canine fossa elongated, but not deep; alveolar process short and prognathic.

NORMA VERTICALIS.—Ovoid, prominent parietal eminences, with minimum frontal diameter of 93 mm., and bizygostephanic index of **69.**

NORMA POSTERIOR.—Well marked pentagonal form. The difference between the asterionic diameter and the maximum breadth is 25 mm.

NORMA LATERALIS.—The frontal curve is regular but rapidly retreating to bregma, where there is a short horizontal plane just posterior to bregma. At obelion the curve passes rapidly downward to a short distance below lambda, which is the occipital point; there is only a very slight break in the region at inion. The zygomatic arches are unusually heavy and short. The alveolar prognathism is pronounced.

NORMA INFERIOR.— Foramen magnum large and elliptical in form, measures 37 x 30 mm. The occipital condyles are long and narrow. There is a well defined protuberance for the jugular process. The left foramen spinosum is unusually large and is bounded posteriorly by the petrous bone.

SUTURES.—The coronal is exceedingly simple; the sagittal and lambdoidal are coarsely denticulated. There are two small wormian bones in both right and left coronal, two in right and left lambdoidal, one at left asterion, two at left pterion and a long narrow bone at right pterion, measuring 29 x 9 mm.

PROCESSES.— Mastoids small; external occipital protuberance fairly indicated. Internal pterygoid plates almost nil. External plates narrow above but broad below; there is no hamular process.

MUSCULAR IMPRESSIONS.— Not so well marked as usual, although the temporal lines are broad and plainly indicated throughout their entire course.

MANDIBLE.— Of small size, condyles narrow and not long, condyloid process long and slender with rather shallow sigmoid notch. Mental eminence weak, but fairly well developed mental tubercles. Height of ramus 64 mm., height of symphysis 34 mm., mandibular angle 130°.

NO. 40,613.—The skull of an adult male of large size and of great weight. Cranial capacity, 1,545 cc. The upper and lower molars, except the upper right third molar and the upper left outer incisor, are *in situ;* the alveoli of the other teeth are present. The floor of the orbital cavity, together with the turbinals and vomer, have been destroyed.

NORMA FRONTALIS.—Forehead retreats beyond the large glabella and projecting superciliary ridges. The minimum frontal width is 100 mm. The orbits are quadrilateral and deep set, with comparatively narrow infraorbital space. The nasal bones are long, broad and highly **arched; the anterior** nasal opening **is** continuous with **the** alveolar **margin, and there is** scarcely any **size to** the nasal spine. The **canine fossa is filled out rather** than **sunken in,** as in the majority of **these skulls.**

Norma Verticalis.— Long **and** narrow, widest throughout the **parietal** eminences. **The frontal** eminences are not largely developed. The anterior external angle **of** the frontal bone is very heavy, and projects to an unusual degree, phænozygous.

Norma Posterior.— Pentagonal **in** form **with** rounded angles **and** converging sides.

Norma Lateralis.—The **deep depression at nasion is striking,** owing to the **prominent development of the** glabella. The curve from ophryon **to obelion is very gradual,** with **a flattening at** the region **of bregma.** The **alveolar arch is** short, and the prognathism is not **as marked as it is in some of the other crania.** Right pterion is **in K.**

Norma Inferior.— **Foramen magnum of elliptical form, measures** 39 x 31 **mm., with the plane directed slightly backwards. Basilar** process **narrow and short.**

Sutures.— **Coronal practically a straight line; the sagittal and** lambdoidal are coarsely serrated. **There is a large irregularly sized** wormian bone just to the left **of lambda, and another in the left lamb-** doidal just above asterion.

Processes.— Mastoids massive **and rough, but not** long. Inner **and outer pterygoid plates** small with **very slight** pterygoid **notch.** The mandibular condyles **are very** broad, **measuring 32** mm.

Muscular Impressions.— Of slight **development for** a male skull **of** such large size. **The external** occipital protuberance **is** fairly well **indicated, but the occipital** lines are scarcely **distinguishable.**

NO. 40,609.— **Cranium** of **adult male, of small cranial** capacity— 1,275 **cc., but massive,** and of **considerable weight—1** pound 13 ounces. **The lachrymal of the right side and the entire inner** side of the left orbital **cavity, together with the turbinals and** vomer, have been destroyed. **Both right and left third molars have** disappeared, **and** their alveoli **are** completely **destroyed.** All **the** other teeth, except the upper and lower incisors, **are** *in situ,* **and** show very **little** evidence of wear. The incisor alveoli **are all** in perfect condition.

Norma Frontalis.— Glabella of enormous size, superciliary ridges **strongly** marked; **orbits** quadrilateral in form; nasal bones of large **size and** heavily **arched,** nasal openings fossa-like, **with** diminutive spine. The canine fossæ are slightly depressed. Malar tuberosities prominent, and zygomatic arches outstanding.

NORMA VERTICALIS.—Oval in outline, with prominènt parietal tubera but very slight frontal development. The temporal fossæ are broad and deep, the superior temporal line passing within 45 mm. of the sagittal suture, just behind bregma. The bizygostephanic index is 78.

NORMA POSTERIOR.—Of well marked pentagonal form, with straight sides and broad base; the asterionic diameter is 116 mm., as compared with 131 mm. for the maximum cranial breadth.

NORMA LATERALIS.—The depression at nasion is very striking, owing to the excessive development of the glabella. The forehead retreats very rapidly behind ophryon and the apex of the curve is reached about 40 mm. posterior to bregma. The occipital squama is almost vertical.

NORMA INFERIOR.—Foramen magnum slightly rounded, measures 33 x 29 mm.; basilar process short and narrow.

SUTURES.—Coronal exceedingly simple; sagittal and lambdoidal coarsely serrated. Synostosis has partially taken place in the coronal below pterion and in the posterior third of the sagittal. There is a small wormian bone in the lower left lambdoidal and one in the lower temporo-parietal suture near asterion.

PROCESSES.—The mastoids are exceptionally massive and rough; the external occipital protuberance is very large and is expanded laterally into a torus occipitalis transversus.

The external pterygoid plate has a broad lateral expansion, with long sphenoidal spines. Especially massive and prominent is the frontal external angular process.

MUSCULAR IMPRESSIONS.—The temporal lines are prominent and broad, with strong ridges on the mandibular angle.

LOWER JAW.—Strong and clean cut. Mandibular angle 112°. Symphysial height, 35 mm.

B. FEMALE CRANIA.

NO. 40,607.—Skull of adult female. The right and left lachrymal and the left òs planum of the ethmoid bone, together with the turbinals and vomer, have been destroyed. Cranial capacity 1,275 cc. The teeth present are well formed, in perfect condition and but very slightly worn. The upper right third **molar and** both lower **third** molars are suppressed.

NORMA FRONTALIS.—(See Pl. V, Fig. 1.) **The forehead** is small but rounded and fairly prominent, and in proportion to **the** face seems **unusually** large. This is owing **to** the extreme narrowness and short-**ness of the** face as shown **by** the bizygomatic diameter of 109 mm., **and the** nasomental **length of only 96** mm. The orbits are of large size, somewhat elongated and measure 40 x 34 mm. There **is a** very **marked** inclination to the orbital axes. The nasal bones are **sym-**metrical and well shaped; the bridge is only moderately acute, **there** being a tendency **at** the lower **aspect to** flatness. Nasal openings rounded, with small spine and incisor **crest.** The canine fossæ are broad and sunken. Alveolar arch short and compressed, **the** outline of each alveolar **cavity** being plainly **indicated. There is** a small foramen on **both sides** passing into **the diploe, just** beneath the supraorbital **notch.**

NORMA VERTICALIS.— (See Pl. V, **Fig. 2.) Long and narrow. The cephalic index is 65.** Parietal eminences well marked, **but** not pro-jecting. **There is a slight** depression on each side just anterior to the eminences. **The frontal region is broader than the occipital.**

NORMA POSTERIOR.— **(See Pl. VI, Fig. 1.) Well marked pentag-**onal form, with prominent **vertex, long almost straight sides and** slightly downward curving base. **The maximum diameter exceeds** the asterionic diameter **by** only **15 mm.**

NORMA LATERALIS.—(See Pl. **VI, Fig. 2.) On the frontal bone the anterior** portion of the curve is well formed, but less than half way up **the** line becomes nearly horizontal until near obelion. There is a **slight** depression **just** anterior to bregma, which is the highest point of the vertex. **From** obelion the curve takes a rapid downward **course** to a **point a**bout 15 mm. above inion. From inion to opisthion **the line is nearly** horizontal. There is a slight depression at nasion, and considerable facial prognathism, with **an** unusual amount of alveolar prognathism. The temporal suture **is** not highly curved. Left pterion in **K.** Right temporal **is removed** from the frontal bone by 6 mm.

NORMA INFERIOR.—(See Pl. III, Fig. 2.) Foramen magnum is slightly rounded **and is rather** larger than one would expect in a skull **of this** capacity; measures 33 x 30 mm. Just anterior to basion and in a **median** line is a well formed third condyle. It is about 6 mm. in height and 7 mm. in breadth. The condyle of the left side is 4 mm. farther forward than **that of the** right side. The palate is long and narrow, in outline U-shaped.   The digastric and occipital grooves are in common; the mastoid foramina are absent.

SUTURES.—The coronal suture is exceedingly simple except just above stephanion for a short distance, where it is slightly denticulated.   The sagittal and lambdoidal sutures are moderately complex. There are two small wormian bones in the lower right lambdoidal, one in the right masto-occipital just below asterion, and one in the temporo-parietal just above asterion, and one in the left masto-occipital just below asterion.

PROCESSES.— Mastoids are small nipple-like projections; styloids small.   The sphenoidal spines are long; one on the left side extends back over the petrous bone, on the right it forms a crest for some length and projects inwards over the foramen spinosum.   The internal pterygoid plates are short and small, the external pterygoids approach to within 5 mm. of the internal ramus of the lower jaw.

MUSCULAR IMPRESSIONS.—The surface of the skull is generally smooth.   The temporal lines, however, can be made out in their entire course.   The inner and outer surfaces of the mandibular angle are rough.

MANDIBLE.—Strong, compact, but small.   There is practically no mental protuberance nor any indication of mental tuberosities.   The mental foramina have their opening directed backwards.   Internal oblique line prominent.   The angles of the mandible converge in a remarkable manner and are only 61 mm. apart, as compared with a distance of 70 mm. from the inner surface of one condyle to the other. Height of ramus, 57 mm.; height of symphysis, 27 mm.; mandibular angle, 128°.

NO. 40,612.— Skull of adult female.   Both zygoma have been broken, and the lachrymals, ethmoids, turbinals and vomer were destroyed in the bandaging of the jaws.   The cranium is rather heavy and has a capacity of 1,345 cc.   The teeth are all *in situ*, in perfect condition and slightly worn; except the upper and lower right inner incisors, the alveoli of which contain plugs of wood.

NORMA FRONTALIS.—(See Pl. VII, Fig. 1.)   The frontal tubera are well developed, very slight glabella and but little indication of superciliary ridges.   The orbits are circular and very slightly higher than wide, index 102.   Deep canine fossæ.   Face long and narrow.

NORMA VERTICALIS.— Oval, the parietal as well as the frontal tubera being strongly marked.

NORMA POSTERIOR.—The pentagon is not as well marked as usual, for the superior angle is extremely open and the base is not depressed

FIELD COLUMBIAN MUSEUM.   ANTHROPOLOGY, VOL. II.

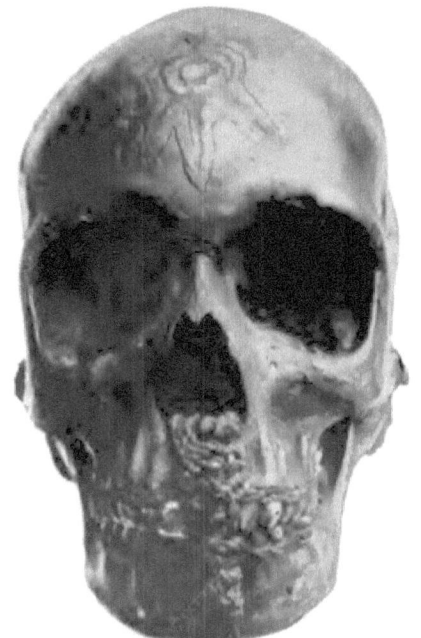

FIG. 1.

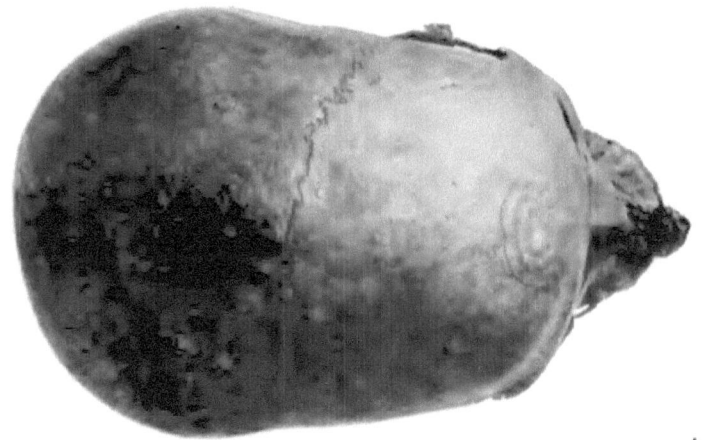

FIG. 2.

PL. V. TWO VIEWS OF FEMALE SKULL, NO. 40,607.

between the mastoids, but projects downwards. There is only 30 mm. difference between the maximum diameter and the asterionic diameter.

NORMA LATERALIS.— (See Pl. VII, Fig. 2.)   Forehead prominent and vertex somewhat flattened, as is also the region just above lambda; below lambda the curve passes forward more gradually than usual. The fronto-nasal depression is very slight.   Alveolar prognathism very pronounced.   Both right and left pterion are formed by a broad frontal process of the temporal bone joining the frontal to the extent of 10 mm.

NORMA INFERIOR.—Foramen magnum is nearly circular, 34 x 30 mm. The condyles are far forward and have a deep backward inclination. The right jugular process extends downwards in a rounded nipple-like projection for about 6 mm.

SUTURES.— Coronal exceedingly simple, sagittal and lambdoidal rather complex.   Synostosis has set in about pterion and throughout the sagittal suture.   There is a medium size wormian bone to the right of lambda.

PROCESSES.— Mastoids very small, and very narrow pterygoids.

MUSCULAR IMPRESSIONS.— Faint, except the inner and outer borders of the angle of the mandible.   Occipital lines scarcely visible.

LOWER JAW.— Rather small but firmly fashioned.   Long coronoid process and broad sigmoid notch.   Ramus broad.   Mandibular angle 115°.

NO. 40,611.— Skull of an adult female, of small size but thick and heavy; capacity 1,060 cc.   The teeth are all present, in perfect condition and but little worn; except the upper incisors and left canine, and the lower left lateral incisor, canine and first premolar which have been lost ; their alveoli are open.   In addition to the normal number of teeth, a lower *left third premolar* has partially erupted between the second premolar and the first premolar.   No trace of it can be seen on the labial surface and it is likely that when completely erupted it would have been forced in between the buccal surfaces of the above mentioned teeth.   Only the crown of the tooth can be seen; it is of normal size.   The ethmoids and vomer have been destroyed.   The right zygoma is broken.

NORMA FRONTALIS.—The orbits are squarish, with nearly perfectly straight axes.   The infraorbital space is disproportionately broad. The nasals are large and flattened, nasal openings are rounded and the nasal spine is insignificant.   The canine fossæ are well marked but not deep. The minimum breadth of the forehead is 91 mm. The nasal index is 60, which is excessively high even for a Papuan. The forehead rises from the face to a considerable height, and the frontal curve is more gradual than it is among the other female skulls of this group.

NORMA VERTICALIS.—The frontal eminences are fairly well developed and compensate in a manner those of the parietal, thus giving the skull an elliptical outline. A slight contraction is noticeable at the sides, along the coronal suture. The posterior half of the skull presents a perfectly symmetrical curve. Bizygostephanic index 81.

NORMA POSTERIOR.— Pentagonal, with rather sharp vertex and converging sides; the maximum breadth exceeds the asterionic diameter by 32 mm. The backward position of the parietal eminences is very striking.

NORMA LATERALIS.—There is a well marked frontal curve due to the frontal eminences, the curve is then very gradual to obelion, where it rapidly passes downward to inion, when it changes abruptly forward. There is a slight elevation at glabella but no perceptible superciliary ridge. The naso-frontal depression is slight; prognathism is confined to the jaws The curve of the temporo-parietal suture from pterion to the termination of the supra-mastoid crest is exceedingly slight.

NORMA INFERIOR.— Foramen magnum is elliptical in shape and measures 30 x 25 mm. There is a double interest in the hard palate: first the median portions of the palatine plates have encroached upon the maxillary bones, and, as a consequence, the transverse palatine suture, instead of being straight as is usual, is irregularly oblique on each side; second, there is a broad, well defined *torus palatinus* extending from the anterior palatine foramen to the maxillo-palatine suture. Just anterior and internal to each foramen ovale is the anomalous foramen of Vesalius. The jugular processes are more than usually well developed.

SUTURES.—The coronal is exceedingly simple throughout its entire length. The sagittal and lambdoidal are rather complex. Synostosis has taken place in all the sutures in the region of pterion. There are no wormian bones.

PROCESSES.—Mastoids small; external occipital protuberance very slightly projecting.

MUSCULAR IMPRESSIONS.—Faintly marked except the occipital curved lines. The internal pterygoid insertion is rougher than that for the masseter muscle.

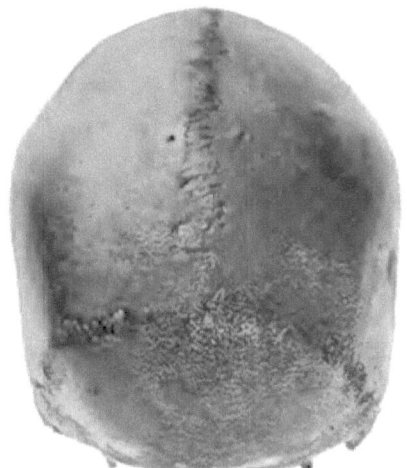

FIG. 1.

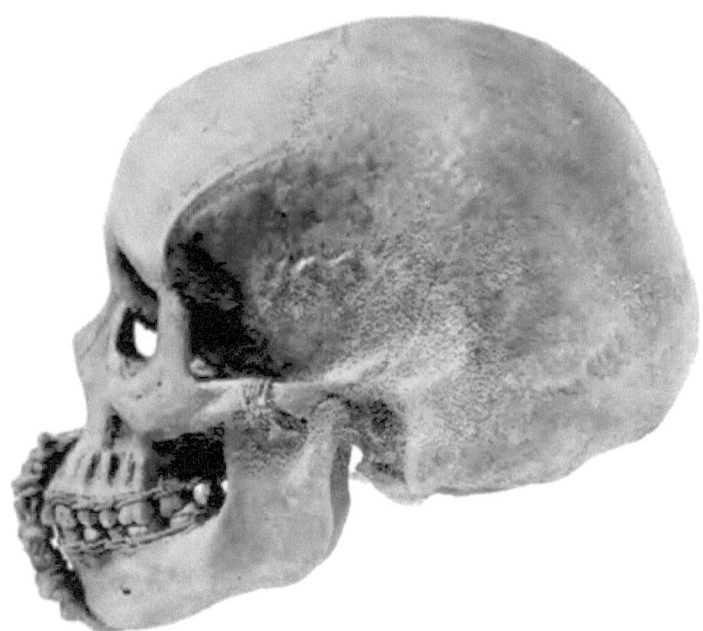

FIG. 2.

PL. VI.   TWO VIEWS OF FEMALE SKULL, NO. 40,607.

LOWER JAW.—Weakly developed. Body narrow and thin; mandibular angle open; mental projection slight; height of symphysis 25 mm.

NO. 40,616.—Skull of adult female. The cranium is large and well formed; capacity 1,345 cc. The lachrymals, ethmoids and vomer have been destroyed. The left upper third molar has never erupted. Of the lower jaw the left, second and third and the right third molars have disappeared, and the alveoli are entirely absorbed. The alveolus of the right upper third molar shows that tooth to have been in an atrophied condition. The upper right second molar and first premolar and the left second molar, together with the lower right first molar and left second and third molars are in situ. None of the alveoli are absorbed. The teeth present are somewhat worn, especially the lower right molar, which has been ground down from before backwards.

NORMA FRONTALIS.— Forehead retreats from the face; very slight glabella. The orbits are squarish with a noticeable droop to the axes. The infraorbital region is broad. The nasals are broad and the inter-nasal and naso-frontal and naso-maxillary sutures are synostosed. The nasal openings are rounded, with very weak nasal spine. Canine fossæ fairly deep. The form of the face is nearly square.

NORMA VERTICALIS.—Parietal eminence prominent. Phænozygous.

NORMA POSTERIOR.— Pentagonal in form, but nearly as broad as high. Superior angle very open.

NORMA LATERALIS.— Both right and left pterion are formed by a broad frontal process of the temporal bone. The curve of the temporo-parietal suture is very slight and quite the opposite from the European type. Forehead is low but curves backwards gradually, flattened over vertex, with strong occipital development between lambda and external occipital protuberance, which shows strongly in profile. The superciliary ridges are slight, with scarcely any naso-frontal depression. Marked alveolar prognathism.

NORMA INFERIOR.— Foramen magnum of oval form, with the condyles far forward; measures 39 x 33 mm. Its plane has a slight backward inclination. The foramen ovale is of exceptional size, that of the left side measuring 9 x 5 mm. External pterygoid plates broad, inner correspondingly narrow. Palate shallow.

SUTURES.—Very simple (No. 2 of Broca's scale). The coronal suture below stephanion is completely effaced. This is almost the condition of the posterior four-fifths of the sagittal and nearly all of the lambdoidal. There are three large wormian bones at lambda;

and three in the left and four in the right lambdoidal suture. There
is also a cluster of wormian bones at both right and left asterion.
The malo-maxillary and spheno-frontal sutures are synostosed.

PROCESSES.— Mastoids are small nipple-like projections, much
compressed from side to side. The styloids have been broken out.
Superior curved line and inion strongly developed for a female
skull.

MUSCULAR IMPRESSIONS.— Not strongly marked except frontal portion of superior temporal line and the region of the masseter of the
mandible.

LOWER JAW.—Mandibular angle, 115°; coronoid process sharp
and long; height of symphysis, 30 mm.

NO. 40,608.— Cranium of adult female. The left zygomatic arch
is broken, as well as the lachrymals, turbinals, ethmoids and vomer.
The cranium is small, round and smooth. Cranial capacity, 1,170 cc.
All the molars of both jaws and the upper first premolars and second
incisors and lower right second premolar are *in situ*. The alveoli of
the other teeth are open. The teeth are not worn and are sound and
perfect. Dental index, 45.

NORMA FRONTALIS.— Forehead narrow and retreating, orbits rect.
angular, with infraorbital suture on right and left side. Nasal bones
of unequal size, broad and flat; nasal opening rounded, with diminutive anterior nasal spine. Canine fossæ not depressed. Malars flattened and appressed.

NORMA VERTICALIS.— Ovoid outline sharply defined, with prominent
parietal eminences placed far back. Dish-like depression at lambda.
The bi-zygostephanic index can not be determined.

NORMA POSTERIOR.— Pentagonal with longest dimensions at sides;
angle at vertex very slight.

NORMA LATERALIS.— Frontal tubera not prominent. Marked facial
and alveolar prognathism. Glabella rounded but no trace of superciliary ridges. Naso-frontal depression very slight. Pterion almost
in K. Zygoma (left) thin and delicate.

NORMA INFERIOR.— Foramen magnum diamond shaped, with condyles very far forward; measures 32 x 28 mm. Deep condyloid fossæ.
Foramen spinosum and foramen ovale have a long, common slit-like
opening, with the apex of the petrosal for a posterior boundary.

SUTURES.—Exceedingly simple in region of bregma and pterion.
The sagittal and lambdoidal are somewhat complex. There is a
small wormian bone just below the left asterion, and several tiny
ossicles in the left lambdoidal suture.

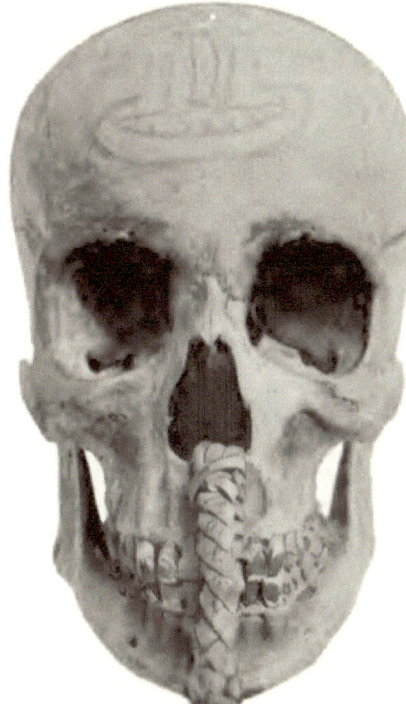

FIG. 1.

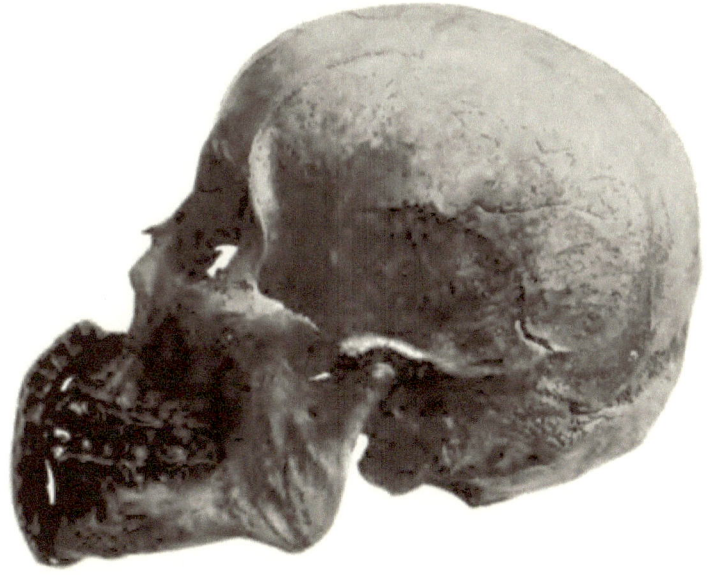

FIG. 2.
PL. VII.   TWO VIEWS OF FEMALE SKULL, NO. 40,612.

Processes.— Mastoids small.   External occipital protuberance **not** indicated.   **Both pterygoid** plates almost absent.

Muscular Impressions.—Very slight.   Occipital lines barely distinguishable.

No. 40,615.—Cranium **of a** young female.   All the teeth have erupted, including the third molars, but the basilar synchondrosis is open.   The teeth are **all large, well** formed, and there is no **trace of wear.**   The upper **right and the** lateral left incisors **are** lost.   Cranial capacity, 1,365 cc.

Norma Frontalis.—(See Pl. VIII, Fig. 1.)   The frontal region is very narrow—minimum width, **89** mm.—with a faintly indicated glabella, but no **trace of** superciliary ridges.   The orbits are rectangular in form, with infraorbital suture **on left side.**   The nasal bones are small, somewhat flattened and of unequal size.   The slope of the nasal opening **is very marked,** and the **nasal** spine is almost nil.   The canine fossæ are **deep.**

Norma Verticalis.— Ovoid shaped.   The narrowness of the frontal region is striking.   Parietal eminences are beautifully indicated **and are situated well back; that of the right side, however, is about 10** mm. anterior **to that of the left.**

Norma Posterior.—(See Pl. VIII, Fig. 2.)   Pentagonal in form, higher than broad and narrowed below.   **The superior curved line is** hidden from view.

Norma Lateralis.—(See Pl. VIII, Fig. 3.)   **Frontal development** is fairly well marked, but the **tubera are not prominent.**   The nasofrontal depression is very slight.   **The** face **is decidedly prognathic, the** alveolar prognathism being very prominent.

Norma Inferior.— Foramen magnum rounded; prominent jugular processes, with deep condyloid fossæ.

Sutures.— Nos. 2–3 **of** Broca's scale.   No wormian bones.

Processes.— Mastoids small **and sharp, but** much compressed from side to **side, and deep** digastric **groove.**   No external occipital protuberance.

Muscular Impressions.— Occipital ridges scarcely visible.   Superior temporal line well **marked but** not situated high **up.**   Insertion **areas** of sterno-cleido-mastoid **and splenius** capitus are very rough.

Mandible.—Well developed.   Mandibular angle very open.   Coronoid process long and sharp, **an unusual** condition for a young skull.

No. 40,610.—This skull **is that** of an adult, but whether of male or **female it is difficult to decide.**   It has a glabella and inion of rather

more than the usual female proportions, but its small capacity and
absence of muscular impressions incline me to consider it the skull of
a female, and in the table of measurements it has been so placed.
Cranial capacity, 1,275 cc. The teeth present are in perfect condition
and but very slightly worn; the following have been lost: upper and
lower left lateral incisors and canines. The interior nares have not
been damaged in the tying of the jaws.

NORMA FRONTALIS.—The frontal region is narrow, the minimum
width being 87 mm. The orbits are nearly square, with narrow infraorbital space. There is present the infraorbital suture on both
sides. The nasal bones are long, narrow and not flattened; nasal
opening is slightly rounded, and the spine is poorly developed. The
maxillaries are high and compressed; deep canine fossæ. The general shape of the entire face is long and narrow. The malar tuberosity
is but faintly indicated, and the zygoma are contracted.

NORMA VERTICALIS.— Strongly ovoid, due to excessive development
of parietal eminences; posterior region narrows rapidly but is prolonged backwards toward the upper occipital squama. Frontal
region narrow. Phænozygous.

NORMA POSTERIOR.— Irregularly pentagonal, owing to asymmetrical development of the parietal eminences, that of the right side being
higher up than that of the left. The sides are nearly straight, and
there is only 28 mm. between the maximum breadth of the skull and
the asterionic diameter.

NORMA LATERALIS.—The curve of the vertex is gradual from glabella to near ophryon, where it passes rapidly downwards to inion
and thence forward. Glabella and inion show plainly in profile, but
there is scarcely any superciliary development. The frontal eminences
are not well marked; the parietal eminences are better marked and
are in the plane of the maximum width. There is but little alveolar
prognathism.

NORMA INFERIOR.—Foramen magnum almost circular in shape,
measures 30 x 27. The right petrous bone is defective at the apex, so
that the foramen lacerum appears as a long slit-like opening which
is continuous with inferior opening of the carotid canal. The posterior condyloid foramina are absent. The right jugular fossa is of
exceptional size.

SUTURES.—The sutures are all simple, especially the coronal,
which is almost a straight line. The coronal contains two wormian
ossicles in its left side, and there is a small epipteric at left pterion.

PROCESSES.— Mastoids of medium size. Styloids very insignificant.
The external pterygoid plates are very broad and triangular in

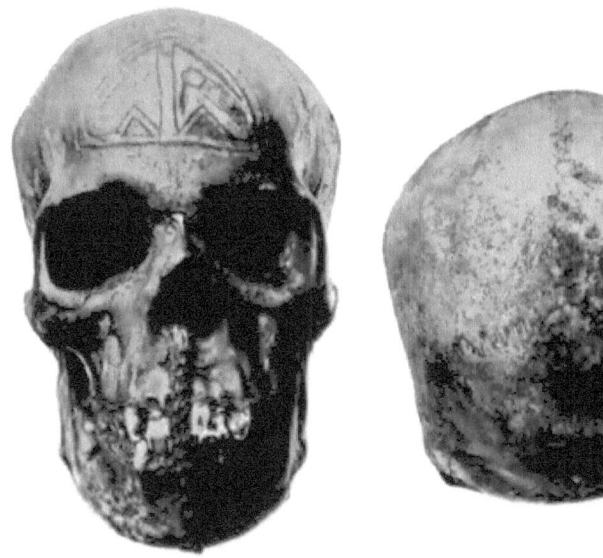

FIG. 1.   FIG. 2.

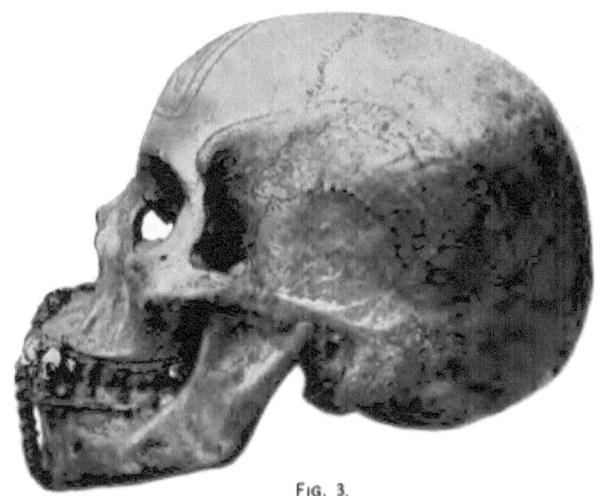

FIG. 3.

PL. VIII. THREE VIEWS OF FEMALE SKULL, No. 40,605.

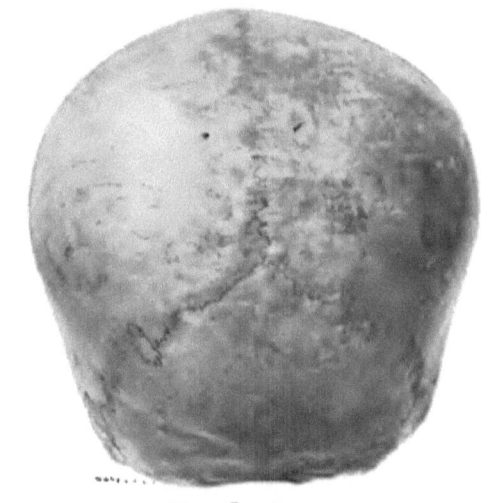

FIG. 1.

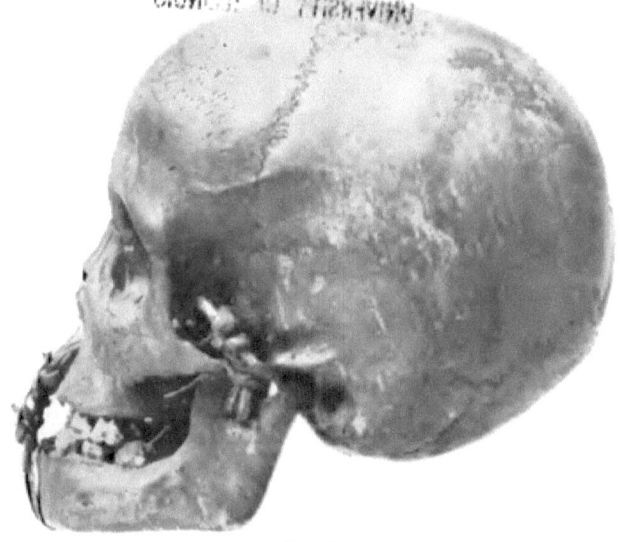

FIG. 2.

PL. X.   TWO VIEWS OF CHILD'S SKULL. NO. 40,606.

shape; internal pterygoids very small.   No hamular process of lachrymals.

MUSCULAR IMPRESSIONS.—The temporal line is broad but not rough or projecting.   The occipital superior curved line is fairly well indicated, and extends from asterion to asterion.   Mylo-hyoid ridge very prominent.

LOWER JAW.—Small and weakly developed.   The mandibular angles converge to a considerable extent.   Mental development small.   Height of symphysis, 30 mm.

C. CHILD'S CRANIUM.

NO. 40,606.—Skull of a child.   Of the permanent teeth, the upper and lower first molars, lower incisors and upper inner incisors have erupted.   The age is, therefore, from 8 to 9 years.   Each of the frontal eminences presents a pathological appearance and is pitted with innumerable small holes.   The parietal eminences also have a somewhat porous or spongy appearance.

NORMA FRONTALIS.—(See Pl. IX, Fig. 1.)   An indication of the glabella can already be made out.   The orbits are high and round, index 100.   The nasal bones are well formed, but there is no bridge as yet; openings rounded.   The frontal development is excessive.

NORMA VERTICALIS.—(See Pl. IX, Fig. 2.)   Ovoid form.   The eminences are all prominent and globular, so that there are no sharp angles in the outline.

NORMA POSTERIOR.—(See Pl. X, Fig. 1.)   Almost circular.   The crown is slightly flattened with narrow base and wide parietals.

NORMA LATERALIS.—(See Pl. X, Fig. 2.)   The forehead rises high and straight above the face; alveolar prognathism slight.

NORMA INFERIOR.—Foramen magnum oval, measures 30 x 24 mm. There are no mastoid foramina, nor are the posterior condylar foramina present.   The left sphenoidal spine is long and hook-like, and is deflected backwards immediately over the foramen spinosum.

SUTURES.—Are all extremely simple.   There is a faint trace of the frontal suture, and a cleft can still be seen from right and left asterion passing out into the occipital bone for a distance of about 10 mm.

MUSCULAR IMPRESSIONS.—The temporal lines are well marked.

PROCESSES.—Mastoids small; external pterygoids already broad with long hamular processes.

PAPUAN CRANIA.

MUSEUM NUMBER	40,617	40,629	40,619	40,618	40,614	40,613	40,609	40,565	Average for Males	40,611	40,616	40,615	40,612	40,610	40,608	40,607	Average for Females	Average for both Sexes	40,006 Child
SEX	♂	♂	♂	♂	♂	♂	♂	♂♂		♀	♀	♀	♀	♀	♀	♀			
CAPACITY	1515	1560	1285	1445	1415	1545	1275	1390	1425	1060	1345	1365	1345	1275	1170	1275	1262	1343	
WEIGHT	30	24	23	24	25	22	29	31	26	20	23	19	18	22	21	21	20	23	
CRANIAL MEASUREMENTS:																			
Glabello-occipital length	191	187	173	174	185	182	179	186	182	166	175	176	164	170	170	179	171	177	161
Maximum breadth	131	140	128	130	107	133	131	122	131	120	133	132	126	128	130	118	127	129	127
Basi-bregmatic height	137	130	130	135	128	134	129	131	131	125	125	131	134	128	120	128	127	129	
Minimum frontal width	103	103	87	93	91	100	95	97	96	91	92	89	89	87	90	95	90	93	
Breadth of base	98	102	94	100	106	96	97	95	98	92	98			95	90	91	94	96	89
Foramen magnum length	36	34	36	37	34	39	33	33	35	30	30	30	34	30	32	33	34	33	82
Foramen magnum breadth	28	32	33	30	28	31	29	28	29	25	33	22	30	27	28	30	27	28	30
Basi-spinal length	96	95	94	92	98	97	101	98	96	91		94	88	89	98	85	90	93	21
Basi-alveolar length	106	105	102	96	107	102	108	106	104	99	127	103	97	95	108	100	100	102	
Bizygomatic breadth		134	122	122	134	125	134	126	128	120	111	117		121		109	118	123	105
Bistephanic breadth	90	105	91	91	104	113	102	110	100	98	75	101	94	99	100	104	101	100	51
Naso-alveolar length	72	72	74	70	71	66	73	77	72	65	113	69	71	70	72	65	69	70	93
Naso-mental length	119		117	115	113	110	119	115	115	101		112	114	113	105		107	111	42
FACIAL MEASUREMENTS:																			
Nasal height	52	47	53	55	49	51	54	51	51	46	56	42	51	50	50	47	49	50	20
Nasal width	27	28	25	27	26	24	27	25	26	28	27	26	26	25	27	25	26	26	32
Orbital width	39	42	35	40	39	40	41	37	39	38	38	39	37	35	38	47	35	37	32
Orbital height	33	34	40	35	32	33	33	35	34	35	38	33	38	33	35	34	35	34	
Dental length	42			38			44	43	41	46		47	41	42	45	44	41	42	
Basi-nasal length	105	101	94	95	94	99	104	98	98	91	96	98	97	95	96	97	96	97	
INDICES:																			
Cephalic	68	74	73	74	71	72	73	65	71	72	76	75	76	77	76	65	73	72	78
Vertical	71	67	74	77	68	73	72	70	71	75	71	75	81	75	70	70	73	72	
Gnathic	110	110	111	104	109	105	106	107	107	108		109	110	106	110	117	110	108	
Upper Facial			60	57	53	52	54	61	55	54	59	59		57			57	56	
Total Facial	53	53	95	98	92	88	89	90	91	84	88	95		93		59	89	90	47
Nasal	51	59	47	49	53	51	50	49	51	60	48	60	50	90	50	53	53	52	100
Orbital	84	83	87	87	86	80	80	94	84	90		84	102	94	90	80	91	87	
Dental	40			40			42	43	41	49	100	48	42	35	45	45	45	43	

GENERAL SUMMARY.

It may not be without interest to note in the first place that in no skull was there a metopic suture, a divided malar bone, or an inter-parietal bone, nor was there any sign of disease or any pathological condition, unless we except that of the child's skull. Furthermore there is no evidence whatever that any of the skulls have ever been subjected to artificial deformation. The skulls, as a rule, are small, compact and heavy. The average weight of the skull, including the lower jaw, is 26 ounces for the males, and 20 ounces for the females; the range being 22 to 31 ounces for the males, and 18 to 23 ounces for the females, a difference between the two sexes so great and so constant as to possess considerable value. The average cranial capacity for the two sexes is 1,343 cc. The average for the males is 1,425 cc., with a range of variation from 1,275 cc. to 1,560 cc.; the average for the female is 1,262 cc., with a range of 1,060 cc. to 1,365 cc. An examination of the table reveals the fact that there seems to be no correlation between the weight of the skull and its cranial capacity. Thus, in the male series the skull with a capacity of 1,545 cc. weighs only 22 ounces, while the skull with a capacity of 1,390 cc. weighs 31 ounces. Similar observations could be made from the female skulls. The capacity as given above is slightly greater than that given by Hovelacque and Hervè for Papuans of New Guinea: they give 1,350 cc. for the males, and 1,250 cc. for the females. According to the above figures, the average sexual differ-ence in the capacity is 165 cc. The skulls as a whole are micro-cephalic, although only two of the male series would fall into that group, the remaining ones being mesocephalic, with three in the megacephalic group. But one female skull is mesocephalic.

NORMA FRONTALIS.—The frontal region varies considerably, natu-rally, in the two sexes. In the males it is narrow, not high, and generally very retreating. The female frontal region is broader and slightly vertical, owing to the frequent strong development of the frontal eminences. In no case, even in the females, does the frontal development assume any considerable vertical height, and in two at least of the females the backward inclination is more marked than it is in some of the male crania. The average minimum frontal width for the males is 96 mm. with a range of variation from 87 to 103 mm.: the average for the females is 90 mm. the variation ranging from 87 to 95 mm.

The glabella is, as a general rule, strongly developed in the males and barely indicated in the females. Often, however, in the males the prominence of the glabella is entirely overshadowed by the strong development of the supraorbital ridges. The latter are even less faintly marked in the females than is the glabella. The sides of the orbit are generally thin and sharp and straight, thus forming a squarish or quadrilateral outline, the former prevailing in the females, the latter in the males. We may expect, therefore, to find some difference in the orbital index for the two sexes. This average is 84 for the males, with a maximum index of 94 and a *minimum* index of 80; the average for the seven females is 91, with 102 for the maximum and 80 for the minimum. The males thus fall into the mesoseme group, while the females belong to the megaseme group. The average for both sexes is 87, which corresponds pretty well to the average of Papuans measured by Turner, but is higher than the average given by Quatrefages and Hamy. The interorbital space varies in width in individual skulls but it certainly averages more than in the European races. The angle of the axes of the orbits also varies greatly in the individual crania. I have measured it in several cases and find it in a few instances to exceed 15°. In the fifteen skulls the infraorbital suture is found on both sides six times, equally divided between the two sexes. This anomalous suture, as Turner has shown, is simply the survival of a fissure which is always present in early life but which normally becomes obliterated.

I have already remarked that in a majority of skulls the lachrymals and ethmoid bones have been destroyed. In five skulls the lachrymals are present. They are generally small, deep set and possess only a slight hamular development. In one case, however, the process reaches the face, while in another case it is absent altogether.

The nasal bones are subject to considerable variation; in some skulls they are broad, even and symmetrical, in others they are small, triangular in shape and very unsymmetrical. The lower margins are in the majority of the skulls more or less damaged. Partial obliteration of the nasal structure occurs twice. The angle formed by the nasal bones varies greatly in the different skulls. In a few instances the angle is decidedly open, so that there is no well formed nasal bridge; in others the bridge is sharp and prominent. The crest of the nasal bridge is concave above, with a slight convexity toward the inferior extremity. In no single case can the lower margin of the nasal opening be said to be sharp. It is either round, or in a few cases sloping, so that the openings are directed almost downwards. The nasal spine is invariably of weak development and small propor-

tions. In a few instances there is a well marked incisor crest. The
mean nasal index for eight males is 51, varying from 47 to 59; for the
seven females the mean is 53, the range being from 48 to 60. The
mean general index for the entire series is 52, thus just coming within
the mesorhine group. This also agrees with Prof. Turner's results,
but is considerably less than the figure given by Hovelacque and
Hervè, which is 54.9.

In a great majority of skulls the canine fossæ are deep, even in
some few examples cavernous. I am not able to detect any sexual
difference in this respect, the variation apparently being wholly individual. The alveolar process of the facial surface of the maxillary
bones has, as a rule, an impoverished, compressed appearance, so
that the eminences produced by the fangs of the teeth stand out in
relief; in many skulls they are so clean cut and well defined that the
exact course of the fangs of all the teeth can be made out.

I have not taken the inter-malar breadth, but have made a comparative examination of the shape, size, etc., of the malar bones. On
the whole they have the appearance of being slightly undersized.
They are not especially prominent, and have sharp, thin borders. In
the males the tuberosity is well defined and projecting; quite the
reverse is true of the females. The average bizygomatic diameter for
the entire series is 123 mm. There is considerable difference between
the two sexes; in the males the mean is 128 mm., maximum 134
mm., minimum 122 mm. In the females the mean is 118 mm., maximum 127 mm., minimum 109 mm. I have no measurement which
equals that of 140 mm. of Prof. Turner, while on the other hand I
can find nothing in his figures which compares with my minimum of
109 mm. This diameter comes from a female skull which is only
remarkable otherwise for its extreme amount of alveolar and dental
prognathism.

For reasons already given I have begun both facial-height diameters at nasion. The mean naso-alveolar length is 70 mm. The
average male length is 72 mm., maximum 77 mm., minimum 66 mm.;
the average for the females is 69 mm., maximum 75 mm., minimum
65 mm. The maximum length given by Turner is 68 mm. In seven
of the eight males the naso-mental length could be taken; this ranged
from 110 mm. to 119 mm., with an average of 115 mm. In the seven
females the mean is 107 mm., with a maximum of 114 mm., and a
minimum of 96 mm. From the bizygomatic diameter and the naso-
alveolar length we get the index of the upper or true face. This
varies from 52 to 61, with a mean of 55 for the males and from 54 to
59 with mean of 57 for the females, thus making the average index

for the entire series 56. This gives a face which is not extremely broad nor extremely narrow, and which may be properly characterized as mesoprosopic. It was possible to compute the total facial index in six males and five females. The results are: For the males, average 91, maximum 96, minimum 88; for the females, average 89, maximum 95, minimum 84. The average for both sexes is 90, which again comes within the mesoprosopic division.

In determining the gnathic index I have compared the basi-spinal to the basi-alveolar length after the method of Prof. Flower,* except, it will be noted, that I have used as the standard the basi-spinal rather than the basi-nasal length. This gives a more accurate expression of what Topinard calls the true prognathism, or alveo-subnasal prognathism. The data are present, however, in the table to compute the basi-nasal basi-alveolar relationship. As the basi-spinal length is taken as 100, the higher the index the greater is the basi-alveolar length, and so, consequently, the greater is the amount of prognathism. The average index for the males is 107, minimum 104, maximum 111; for the females the average is 110, minimum 106, maximum 117. The mean general gnathic index for the entire series is 108; this represents an extreme amount of prognathism which is probably not surpassed by that of any other race. Furthermore, this does not represent the full prognathic character of this series of crania, for it leaves out of consideration the teeth, which in many cases project forward at an angle of 20°–40°.

NORMA VERTICALIS.—The skulls are, as a rule, long and narrow, with compressed frontal region, fairly well developed parietal eminences which are usually situated pretty well back. There is a marked difference between the two sexes in the dimensions. Thus, the average maximum length in the male is 182 mm., in the female the average is 171 mm. The longest cranium measured is 191 mm., that of a male; the shortest is 164 mm., belonging to a female. The average maximum width of the male crania is 131 mm., of the female 127 mm. The range of variation for the entire series is from 118 mm. to 140 mm. Adopting the classification of Prof. Flower for the cephalic index, it appears that the male crania are, without a single exception, dolichocephalic, having a mean index of 71, with a maximum of 74 and a minimum index of 65, the series as a whole being remarkably uniform. There is even more uniformity in the indices of the seven females, with the exception of one skull which has the low index of 65. The other six range from 72 to 77, and average 75, and

* " On the Osteology and Affinities of the Natives of the Andaman Islands." Journal of Anthrop. Institute, Nov., 1879, p. 12.

with the addition of the index of 65 the mean total average for the female index is **73.** As the glabella contributes not a little to lower the index in the male cranium, the difference between the two sexes is no more than we should expect to find   The decided dolichocephalism of the entire series is extremely interesting in view of the probability, as shown by Turner, of the existence of a brachycephalic as as well as a dolichocephalic type on the island of New Guinea, and I more than ever regret that the exact locality from which the collection under consideration comes is not known. It may be noted here, however, that the uniformity which generally prevails in the cephalic index, as well as in the other important indices of the cranium, render it extremely likely that the crania are from a single locality. How much light can be thrown on the location of this region by the carvings on the frontal bones remains yet to be seen. It is to be noted in this place also, although I have already briefly alluded to the fact, that there is no evidence of any of the crania having been subjected to artificial pressure, either in the frontal or parieto-occipital region. This fact also helps to circumscribe the territory from which these skulls might have come, as it has been shown that artificial deformation, either in the frontal or parieto-occipital region, is practiced in several parts of the island.

I have taken the bi-stephanic breadth in both the males and females ; it averages 100 mm. and 101 mm. respectively. This diameter compared to the bizygomatic diameter gives* what Topinard has called the bi-zygostephanic or fronto-zygomatic index, and shows the amount of zygomatic projection or greatest cranio-facial width in relation to the fronto-parietal breadth at stephanion, thus forming a good substitute for the so-called angle of Quatrefages. This index for the males is 78, in the females it is naturally higher, 85. The entire series is thus decidedly phænozygous, as opposed to cryptozygous, where the index is above 90. According to the results obtained by Professor Garson and others this index of 78 for the males is the lowest average† recorded for any race except the Eskimo and some other branches of the Papuan group. As will be noted more fully later on the temporal lines are as a rule prominently indicated and often encroach upon the vertex. By comparing my measurements it appears that there is no sexual difference in this respect, and that in at least seven crania the temporal line extends to within less than 50 mm. of the sagittal suture, the variation for the entire series being from 40 to 70 mm.

---

*See especially, Turner : Challenger Reports, Zoology, Vol. X. pp. 85, 86.
†See Journal of Anthrop. Society for 1879-80, and for May, 1891.

NORMA POSTERIOR.— All of the skulls are of pentagonal form, but the outline is varied considerably in the different individuals by a greater or less development of the parietal eminences, and by the angle which the parietal bones make at the sagittal suture. In some cases this is very open; in others it is so sharp as to give a crest-like appearance to the vertex. The sides of the crania are as a rule nearly straight and parallel, so that in many cases the bi-asterionic diameter nearly equals the maximum breadth diameter. The latter diameter is invariably found through the parietal eminences. In only one instance are the parietal eminences unusually prominent, and in this skull the basilar synchondrosis is still open, although the third molars have all erupted. The width of the base of the cranium is remarkably uniform, averaging 98 mm. in the male series and 94 mm. in the female series; the range of variation for the entire series being but 16 mm. Although the data are present in the table, I have not computed the altitudinal index of breadth-height for each individual skull; but comparing the average of these two diameters for the entire series we have a mean general breadth-height index of 100; in other words the basi-bregmatic height and the maximum breadth are equal. In one instance, however, the index is 108. The average breadth-height index for Papuans is put by Topinard at 105.

NORMA LATERALIS.—With but few exceptions the frontal development is weak, the eminences are not strongly marked, and there is consequently very little vertical development in the frontal bone. The highest point of the vertex is situated to a considerable distance behind bregma, while the vertex is, as a general rule, somewhat flattened. The curve downwards from obelion to inion is very rapid, with occasionally a depression, so that the curve is almost straightened out. There is in all instances a well marked occipital development between lambda and the external occipital protuberance, so that in no case does the maximum diameter fall at the external occipital protuberance or below it. In no case, furthermore, is there any pronounced subiniac development, that portion of the occipital bone being extremely shallow and giving but very little depth to the cerebellar fossæ.

The average basi-bregmatic height for the eight males is 131 mm.; the maximum height is 137 mm.; the minimum, 128 mm.; the average for the seven females is 127 mm.; the maximum is 134 mm.; minimum, 120 mm. Combining these averages with the glabello-occipital length we have a mean vertical or length-height index for the males of 71; the average for the females is, as might be expected, a trifle higher, 74. The highest vertical index is in a female skull,

81; the lowest is 68, from a male.   Adopting the nomenclature of Turner,* we may say the series is very slightly metriocephalic, or, in the German nomenclature, orthocephalic.   It may be noted in the table that the mean general vertical index and the cephalic index are about equal.   Of course, this can happen only when the basi-breg-matic height is equal to the maximum transverse diameter.   As Turner has shown, this is not the case in the brachycephalic Papuan crania, but is the rule in the dolichocephalic crania.   If the doli-chocephalism is pronounced the vertical index will exceed the cephalic index, as in fact it does in the majority of the skulls of the present series.

NORMA INFERIOR.—The foramen magnum is ovoid or at times dia-mond shape in outline.   It averages 35 mm. in length in the males and 32 mm. in the females; the average width is 29 mm. for the males and 27 mm. for the females; hence the foramen magnum is larger in the males than in the females.   The basilar process is short and relatively narrow.   The condyles are, as a rule, well forward, and in some instances encroach on the anterior median aspect.   There is considerable indi-vidual variation in the size, etc., of the various foramina, the foramen ovale and spinosum especially showing considerable range, and the posterior condyloid foramen being absent in several instances and the fossæ being subject to great variation in size and depth.   In one skull there was platybasic deformation.

For reasons already given it was found impossible to measure or fully describe the hard palate, and this is much to be regretted.   A well marked torus palatinus occurs once, and in two palates the transverse palatine suture is not horizontal but oblique in its course, owing to the encroachment of the median portions of the palatine bones on the maxillary bones.   In no skull was there discovered any trace of a pre-or inter-maxillary suture, but this failure may in part, perhaps, be ascribed to the blackened condition of the palates and also to the fact that careful examination from the inferior surface was impossible.   It was also impossible to make any observations on the depth, width or position of the glenoid fossæ.

LOWER JAW.— No definite series of observations was made on the lower jaw for reasons already given, but its weak development is very noticeable.   The mental protuberance and tubercles are rarely strongly marked, while in many instances there is a distinct backward inclination in the symphysis from above downwards.   The ramus may be described as short and narrow, with an extremely open

---

*"Challenger Reports," Zöology. Vol. X. "Human Crania," p. 4.

mandibular angle. The mental spines are, as a rule, very faintly marked. The most striking feature, perhaps, of the whole series is the roughened masseter surface, which, at times, becomes a veritable outward projecting crest at the base of the ramus. This is more noticeable in the males than in the females.

TEETH.— In four male skulls and in six female skulls it was possible to compute the dental index, after the method of Prof. Flower.* The average for the males is 41, with a maximum of 43 and a minimum of 40; the average index for the female series is 45, with a maximum of 49 and a minimum of 42. The mean general index for the series is 43. As the female series is the larger, and hence more accurate, and as Prof. Flower has shown that there is an average of only two points, or even less, between the two sexes, it is highly probable that the mean general index in this series is too low, and that the index of 44 would be more accurate as an index for the group. As it is, the males are in the microdont and the females in the megadont division.

It is a somewhat significant fact that in no skull is there a single unsound tooth, and only in two skulls have any teeth been lost during life. The teeth are invariably good sized, well formed and generally in perfect alignment. As has been described in the preceding section, in two of the lower jaws there is a supernumerary molar, and in three skulls one or both pairs of the third molars have been suppressed. These I have commented upon more fully elsewhere.† The wear of the teeth has been almost nil; in only one case could the wear be said to correspond to No. 2 of Broca's scale.

SUTURES.—The sutures are, as a rule, exceedingly simple. Occasionally, however, the sagittal or lambdoidal suture is very coarsely serrated. In all the skulls there is a gradually increasing amount of complexity in the serration beginning with the coronal and ending with the lambdoidal. There is but little evidence of synostosis, no suture being entirely effaced, and only a very few showing any signs of synostosis at all. Wormian bones occur rather frequently in the lambdoidal suture, the largest one measuring 25 x 30 mm. The largest spheno-parietal suture is 19 mm. In two instances pterion is formed in K. In four it is pterion "retourne"—always by a frontal process from the temporal bone; in four other crania epipteric bones occur at pterion. Thus only one-half of the entire series have pterion formed in the usual manner, in H.

---

* On the Size of the Teeth as a Character of Race. Journal of the Anthrop. Inst., Nov. 1884.

† "Numerical Variations in the Molar Teeth of Fifteen Papuan Skulls." Dental Review, April, 1897, Chicago.

PROCESSES.—The mastoid processes are unusually well developed in the males; poorly developed in the females. But even when they reach their greatest development they by no means attain to the size often found in American crania; they generally have a laterally compressed appearance, and are frequently sharp pointed. The styloid processes have all been destroyed. In many of the crania, especially those of males, the comparative massiveness of the external angular process forms a very striking feature of the face.

MUSCULAR IMPRESSIONS.— Reference has been made, over and over again, to the strongly marked temporal lines; they are almost without exception well developed, and reach high up on the temporal bone towards the vertex. The impressions for the masseter and external pterygoids are also, as a rule, heavily moulded. In the male the external occipital lines and protuberance are strikingly prominent. In many cases the superior curved line forms a strong projecting torus occipitalis transversus, in which inion is entirely overshadowed, but in other skulls inion is prolonged into a large roughened projection.

SUMMARY.—The crania as a whole may be characterized as :

MICROCEPHALIC,	PROGNATHIC,
DOLICHOCEPHALIC,	MESOPROSOPIC,
METRIOCEPHALIC,	MESORHINE,
PHÆNOZYGOUS,	MESOSEME,

MEGADONT (MESODONT).

PRESERVATION AND DECORATIVE FEATURES OF PAPUAN CRANIA, By WM. H. HOLMES.

ORIGIN OF CRANIA.

Our information in regard to the crania described by Dr. Dorsey in the preceding pages merely enables us to locate them in a general way in the island of New Guinea. The sea captain who brought them to this country affirmed (so it is stated) that they were obtained from a native chief, and it is probable that they came from the vicinity of some of the ports of the island. That they came from this island is confirmed by the craniological characters of the specimens, and more especially by their unique embellishments, the latter differing from those of Borneo and other islands from which examples have been secured.

As a matter of course in an island of the great size of New Guinea, there are numerous more or less distinct groups of people, and corresponding groups of art phenomena, and when these become better known there will probably be little difficulty in relegating these skulls to their proper people and province. It seems not unlikely that they are from the northern shores of the Papuan Gulf, in the British protectorate, since the decorative designs seem to affiliate pretty closely with those of this district, as illustrated by Haddon;* and Chalmers describes engraved skulls as commonly preserved in the temples of that locality.

SKULLS OF FRIENDS AND FOES PRESERVED.

It seems pretty well established that skulls of friends as well as of foes were preserved and prized by these peoples, and I get the impression from the care taken of the specimens under consideration, and the tasteful elaboration of the decorative features, that they were the skulls of members of the tribes or families owning them, rather

---

* Haddon, A. C., Decorative Art of British New Guinea, p. 89.

than of enemies. Chalmers is quoted by Haddon as saying that he saw in the temples of the village of Maina "numerous skulls of men, women and children, crocodiles and wild boars, also many breasts of the cassowary. All are carved and many painted. The human skulls are of those who have been killed and eaten. * * * I fancy each man who has killed or helped to kill a foe has his own peculiar painting and carving on the skull."[*] This author suggests that the skulls may have been used as offerings to the wicker images seen in the temples. It is possible that Chalmers' idea that the skulls seen were the skulls of enemies taken in battle was only a guess. I do not have sufficient of the literature of the subject at hand to enter into a discussion of this point, but believe it to be a fact sufficiently well established that among many of the insular peoples skulls of friends and relatives were preserved and revered as sacred relics, and even in cases became the subject of superstitious veneration or worship; and this is certainly much more reasonable than to suppose that any such feelings should extend to the skulls of strangers and enemies. It is undoubtedly true, however, that the skulls of enemies were and still are taken and preserved by these and many other peoples; the reason most commonly given being the belief that they imparted to the possessor some of the enviable qualities of the person represented, beside no end of magic influence. These skulls were used as drinking cups, and may have been thought to impart extraordinary properties to the liquid used. Employed thus and for ceremonial purposes they were probably painted, engraved or otherwise ornamented, but I have difficulty in believing they would be carefully kept intact, preserved with great care and elaborately ornamented as are the skulls here considered.

CARE OF CRANIA.

The preservation of these skulls was evidently a matter of much concern to the owners. It was essential that they should be perfect in every detail. Especial care was taken that no part should be lost. The jaws were secured by fastenings at the right and left and in front. The teeth were carefully tied in and when lost were replaced by artificial teeth made of wood or other material shaped in imitation of the original teeth. This is illustrated in Nos. 40,612, 40,616, 40,614, the much decayed wooden substitutes being still in place.

---

[*] Quoted by Haddon, Decorative Art of British New Guinea, p. 169.

The manner of securing the teeth is illustrated in several of the plates and especially in Pl. XI, which represents a portion of skull No. 40,607. Fig. 1 is intended to show the peculiar knottings or

Fig. 1.   Manner of Looping Cord in Fastening Teeth (Enlarged).

loopings employed. The cord is fastened around the back molar on one side, and carried along, inclosing each tooth in turn, in a loop, making a very effective fastening when the cord is tightly drawn and attached to the back molar of the other side. As indicated in Pl. XI, the teeth (see third upper molar) are held in place even after becoming entirely loose in the sockets. The cord, shown actual size in this plate, is made of palm fiber and is well twisted and even.

The lower jaw was secured at the right and left by heavy twisted cords or palm splints, which were passed several times through a hole drilled in the ramus just below the sigmoid notch and carried over

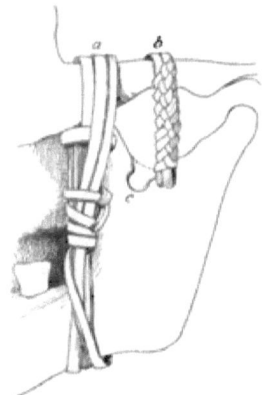

Fig. 2.   Original Fastening, *b*; Broken out at *c*.   Second Fastening Carried Around Jaw, *a*.   ½.

the zygomatic arch. The fastening was completed by binding the strands tightly around the middle portion, as indicated in Fig. 2 and in some of the plates. Fig. 2 illustrates an instance in which the

sigmoid perforation was broken out and the attachment renewed by
passing the splints over the zygomatic arch and all the way down
around the angle of the jaw.

The most striking feature of these fastenings is the band which
extends around the point of the chin and through the nasal passage.
A palm splint or strong cord was carried half a dozen times around
and then bound by loopings of the same strand, as well shown in Figs.
3 and 4 and in several of the plates.   The binding of the strands is in
cases very elaborate and neat, and again very imperfect and slovenly.

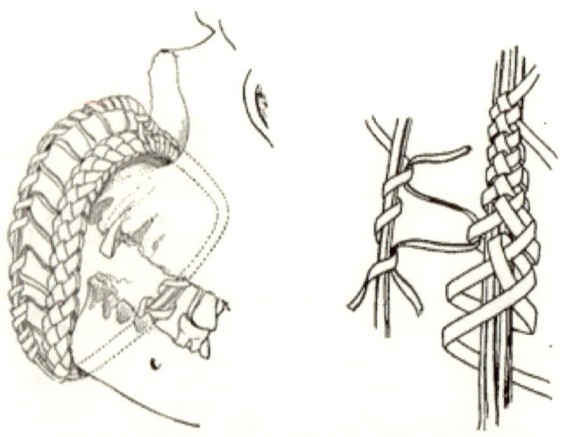

FIG. 3.   JAW FASTENING OF PALM-LEAF SPLINTS. ½.
FIG. 4.   LOOPING OF JAW FASTENING. ½.

In some instances strands were carried through between the teeth,
inclosing and drawing together the inner and outer turns of the fastening, thus effectively tightening the tie.   In cases considerable
trouble has been taken to make these fastenings neat and tasteful in
appearance.   Not only are the looping and tying carefully done, but a
special ornamental feature is added, as seen in Fig. 3 (skull 40,613).

FIG. 5.   JAW FASTENING AND ORNAMENT. ½.   FIG. 6.   ORNAMENTAL TIE OF PALM FIBER. ½.

An outstanding strand is carried around in front of the tie proper, and is held in place by a meandering fillet which passes alternately under the loopings of the adjacent parts of the tie proper and the outstanding band.   An additional embellishment, seen in a few cases, consists of a neat tie of palm fiber fringed at the ends; this encircles the zygomatic arch in front of or behind the lateral jaw fastenings, as seen in Figs. 5 and 6.

Ornamental treatment of jaw fastenings is common among the head hunters of Melanesia.   The work is generally very neat, and many of the peoples show no little skill in the making of cordage and in the employment of woven or plaited fastenings and decorations.

EMBELLISHMENT OF CRANIA.

It is apparent that not only were the crania of this collection cared for in the most scrupulous manner, but that æsthetic consid-erations were of importance.   All the seventeen skulls are decorated with designs engraved on the frontal bone, and in two cases (40,613 and 40,618) the figures extend back over the coronal suture to the parietal bones.   Viewed from the front all are centrally placed, as

Fig. 7. Engraved Design from Skull
No. 40,613. ½.

Fig. 8. Engraved Design
from Skull No. 40,610. ½.

seen in the plates.   In execution the work is not of a high order; the scratchy lines, evidently engraved in the main with a sharp point, straggle about in a haphazard way.   My illustrations, Figs. 7 to 22, engraved one-half actual size, were secured by working over carefully made rubbings with a fine pen point, thus preserving, as far as possible, the scratched effects. Some of the lines are quite deep, but none are regular or even, while the broader areas are, in many cases, worked down slightly all over by scratching and scraping. All the designs are comparatively simple, not embodying more than two or

FIG. 9.   ENGRAVED DESIGN FROM SKULL
No. 40,617. ½.

FIG. 10.   ENGRAVED DESIGN FROM SKULL
No. 40,612. ½.

three elements in any case. It is my impression that all are significant, being totems or having their origin in the crude mythologic conceptions of the people. Nearly all embody easily distinguished animal forms. The more formal examples, approaching the purely geometric, are also doubtless animal derivatives or representations of land, water or other natural phenomena.

FIG. 11.   ENGRAVED DESIGN FROM SKULL
No. 40,595. ½.

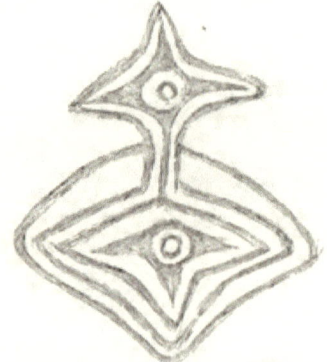

FIG. 12.   ENGRAVED DESIGN FROM SKULL
No. 40,618. ½.

Fig. 13. Engraved Design from Skull No. 40,605. ½.

Fig. 14. Engraved Design from Skull No. 40,614. ½.

Fig. 15. Engraved Design from Skull No. 40,607. ½.

Fig. 16. Engraved Design from Skull No. 40,619. ½.

Fig 17. Engraved Design from Skull No. 40,609. ½.

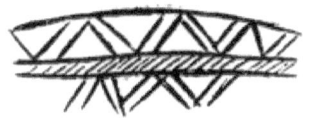

Fig. 18. Engraved Design from Skull No. 40,606. ½.

Fig. 19. Engraved Design from Skull No. 40,608. ½.

FIG. 20.   ENGRAVED DESIGN FROM SKULL
No. 40,620.   ½.

FIG. 21.   ENGRAVED DESIGN FROM
SKULL No. 40,616.   ½.

FIG. 22.   ENGRAVED DESIGN FROM SKULL No. 40,613.   ½.

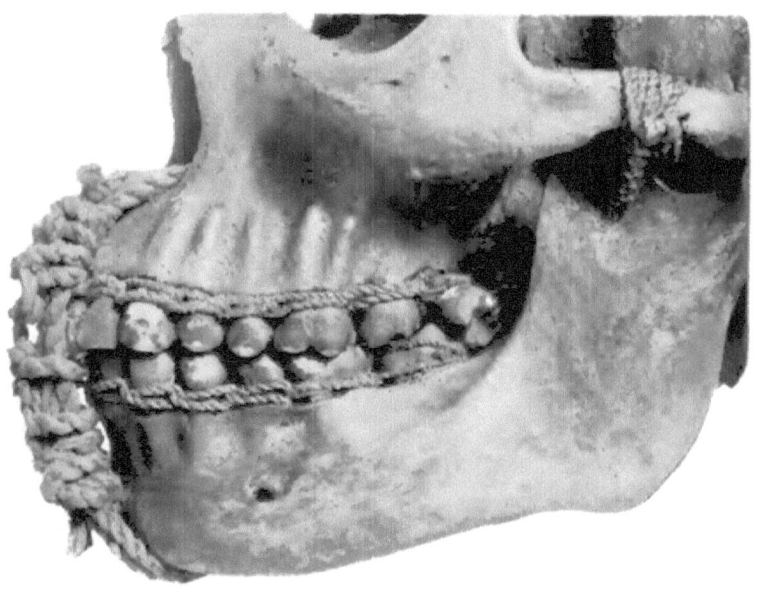

PL. XI. JAW AND TEETH FASTENINGS. FEMALE SKULL, NO. 40,607. ½.

www.ingramcontent.com/pod-product-compliance
Lightning Source LLC
Chambersburg PA
CBHW031244260626
47169CB00007B/2441